Mersh'e

The Magician

Mersh'e

All in the Mind

Mersh'e The Magician is a fairy tale loosely based around the character of the Greek God Hermes, who in turn was derived from the Egyptian God Thoth.

Thoth was the God of wisdom, medicine, astronomy and the moon. He is credited with the creation of the 365 day calendar and associated with writing, learning and magic. As a great magician he was called Hermes Trismegistus, Greek for "Thrice Greatest Hermes."

Once upon a time there lived a great magician. He was three hundred years old and his name was Mersh'e. For the first half of his life, he trained with the greatest of all the magicians, Clavis Arcarna. He learnt the secrets of the plants, the mysteries of the rocks and the songs of the wind.

Then for the next one-hundred-and-fifty years, Mersh'e traveled all over the world, meeting wise men who lived in Egypt, India, China and Persia. When he returned home, he was the wisest of them all.

The King heard about the famous magician Mersh'e from his bluebird messenger and demanded Mersh'e attend the Palace immediately.

When Mersh'e arrived, the King said, "Tell me Magician, what was the most astounding thing you saw on your journey?"

Mersh'e replied, "Oh, your majesty, great and powerful one, it was surely the Oracle of the Shrine in the far-off gardens of Elysium."

Thereafter he described the shrine where the floating head of the oracle rested, surrounded by beautiful hanging curtains and marble pillars.

The King asked, "Of what did the Oracle speak? Perhaps it has heard of my power and fame."

The Oracle had not, Mersh'e assured the King. It had spoken about the beasts of the earth and birds of the sky and how they might be friends and live together happily.

And how with thoughtfulness and kind deeds, life would be enriched. Everyone would share and help each other so there would be no need for money or wealth, greed or cruelty.

When Mersh'e left the palace, he thought how nice the King had been, but the King was feeling far from it. He was furious at Mersh'e for telling him of such ridiculous ideas, such as giving up all the things he dearly loved. What would happen to all of his fine clothes and glorious jewels, his furs, and priceless silks?

The King was so cross he called for his servant to fetch his stallion. He was going to visit the Witch of the Woods, to find a way to stop Mersh'e and stop his words from coming true. When he rode off into the night, he was so full of hatred his brain was on fire and two small horns sprung up on his forehead.

The King spent all night with the Witch of the Woods who was a giant being with hair down to her knees and flaming red eyes. He was very frightened, but determined to keep his kingdom. He watched, full of fear, while she took up a huge wooden wheel and began to chant.

She sang and danced all night until dawn. When the first rays of morning slid across the horizon, Horatio, her snake, slithered up the spokes of the wheel and announced an end to the spell.

Meanwhile, Mersh'e was at home in his castle reading spells when he heard his two dogs making strange sounds outside. He went out and there under the moonlight were his two favorite hounds, dancing and howling under the clear night sky.

"What is it boys?" he asked, and with their barks and growls they told him what the King was up to.

Mersh'e was horrified to hear the King had been so sly and deceptive. He then went inside to prepare for the witch's spell.

Mersh'e waited in silence for the witch's spell. He had no need of potions or tricks as his power came from within. He was without fear and without doubt, because his faith in the universe was greater than any foe. So, when the witch's spell cast Mersh'e into the air, and great bolts of lightning hurtled down on him, he was not fooled. Although his castle was destroyed and the great oak burnt down, Mersh'e knew he could not be harmed because the witch's power was not real.

The Witch of the Wood's spell lasted forty nights, and when it was over the King went to see the destruction that was caused. Nothing was as it had been before. He looked everywhere but could not find Mersh'e. The old oak grew afresh from the life-giving red waters of the moat, and beneath a blazing star shone a face that stared at him with subdued understanding.

"Doest, thou know what thou hast done?" the Oracle of the Oak intoned. "Doest, thou know thou hast sent to another place the greatest magician of all time? Mersh'e could have helped you to live beyond your greed and selfish desires, but you drove him away . . ."

The King wept. He realised the terrible
mistake he had made. Mersh'e had gone
forever, and now he was alone. But,
Mersh'e knew of the King's sorrow, as he
flew above the ruined castle, watching
the clouds, float higher and higher and
higher . . . until he reached the sun.

And there Mersh'e lives to this day, with
his dogs, happy as a King. He shines
down on all the people and the animals
and the plants.

Now he truly is the greatest magician of
them all.

The End

Mersh'e©Sarah Cavill

Written by Sarah Cavill
Illustrated by Sarah Cavill

First Published in Australia 2025
by
Carole Campbell Writer
carolecampbell390@gmail.com

National Library of Australia
Cataloging – in Publication data

Adolescent Fiction
ISBN: 978-0-6487334-7-8

Book Design
By Sarah Cavill
Publisher
Carole Campbell Writer
Produced in Australia